COURAGE can change the World

Tala
The Bengal Tiger

Written by
Beverly Jatwani

Illustrated by
Sunita Chawdhary

NEW FRONTIER PUBLISHING

'Ma,' said Veera, as she ground the spices for the evening's meal,
'Can you tell me the story of when I was born?'

Veera's mother smiled. She had
repeated that story dozens of
times before.

COURAGE *can change*

the World

WILDLIFE VETS INTERNATIONAL

All author royalties from the sale
of this book go to WVI.
www.wildlifevetsinternational.org

For my strong and courageous dad,
who is forever in our hearts. ~ B J

This book is for Gaurav. ~ S C

This edition published in Great Britain 2022
by New Frontier Publishing Europe Ltd
Uncommon, 126 New King's Road, London, SW6 4LZ
www.newfrontierpublishing.co.uk

First published by Little Steps Publishing 2021

Text copyright © 2021 Beverly Jatwani
Illustrations copyright © 2021 Sunita Chawdhary

The rights of Beverly Jatwani to be identified as the author
and Sunita Chawdhary to be identified as the illustrator of this work have been asserted.

A CIP catalogue record for this book is available from the British Library.

ISBN: 978-1-915167-11-8

Edited by Tasha Evans • Designed by Verity Clark

Printed in Turkey
1 3 5 7 9 10 8 6 4 2

MIX
Paper from
responsible sources
FSC www.fsc.org **FSC® C111584**

'It was a warm summer morning,' Ma began. 'The sun was rising and the village was quiet. Suddenly, your loud cries echoed through the air as I held you for the very first time.'

'At that moment, I looked outside our window and caught a glimpse of a beautiful tiger cub. Its golden fur was the brightest I had ever seen. One of its ears was orange, the other black. It almost looked as if it was there to protect you. I took that as a sign and named you Veera.'
'Because *veer* means courageous!' added the girl, with a smile.

Veera and her family lived in a village in the dense mangrove forest. Most of the mud houses were fenced with fishing nets on bamboo poles, to protect the people and their animals from predators.

chirp
chirp

CROAK!

Every night, the villagers would fall asleep to the sounds
of the jungle — the chirping of crickets, the croaking of
frogs, the rustling of trees . . . and, sometimes, the
clamorous roars of the Bengal tigers.

Veera felt very sad when trees in the mangrove forest were cut down. This jungle was also home to the tigers and other wildlife and the villagers had found ways to peacefully live with these majestic animals.

Whenever Veera heard the tigers' distant roars, or found paw prints on the edge of the village, she found herself thinking of the cub that appeared out of nowhere on the day she was born.

Veera named this cub Tala. She would often
stare at Tala's picture and feel her heart racing.
Although she feared the tiger, she also felt
a strong need to protect them.

RAAAR!

Veera would often find herself thinking about Tala. She would think about
Tala when she walked with her brother to the village school, where they
would sit in the open air under the shade of tall palm trees.

She would think about Tala at lunchtime as she worked with her friends on her plan to 'Save the Tigers'.

She would also think about Tala as she headed home in the afternoon, walking through the colourful alleys.

One Sunday morning, Veera woke up feeling very excited.
'Happy birthday, princess!' said Pa. 'I can't believe you're 10 already!'

Veera smiled. 'Pa, can I come
fishing with you today?" she asked.
'I would love that,' her father replied,
and handed her a fishing rod.

After a short walk through the jungle, Veera and her
father arrived at the riverbank.
'Oh dear!' exclaimed Pa. 'I can't find the bag with the
bait. I must have dropped it along the way. Please wait
here for a moment while I look for it.'

Veera dipped her feet into the cool water of the
river. It felt *so* refreshing on that hot, sunny day,
but something did not feel right.

She looked around, noticing the stillness of the jungle.

A rustle in the bushes caught her attention. She looked through the tall grass and saw the unmistakable black and gold stripes of a Bengal tiger.

Time stopped as the tiger and
the girl stared at each other.

Overcome by fear, Veera was
unable to move.

Next came the deepest and loudest roar she had
ever heard as the tiger leapt towards her.

Veera crouched down with her arms on her head,
waiting for the worst to happen.

RRRR!!!

A few seconds passed by before Veera found the courage
to open her eyes again. What she saw next left her speechless.

The tiger jumped past her towards a crocodile that
was just a few steps behind Veera, ready to attack.

ROARRRRRRRRRR!!!

Scared by the tiger's roar, the crocodile splashed
back into the water. It then swam to the marshes
on the other side of the river.

Veera stared in disbelief. How was it
possible that the tiger had just risked
its own life to protect her?

Her eyes met the eyes of the tiger, who was now sitting just a few metres from her. Its golden fur was the brightest she had ever seen, and its ears looked almost familiar – one was orange, one was black.

Veera's heart skipped a beat. There, in front of her, was Tala, the tiger that had mysteriously appeared near her home exactly ten years ago, on the day she was born.

'Veeraaa!' Pa was shouting in the distance – he had heard
Tala's roar. As he got closer, Tala stood up, gave Veera one
last look and disappeared among the bushes.
'Goodbye, my friend,' whispered Veera.

Just then something shiny
caught her eye, glinting in the
grass where Tala had been.

Veera picked it up. It was a token in the shape of a puzzle piece, with the word COURAGE written across it.

Veera held the token tightly in her hand. 'Thank you for teaching me what courage means,' she said, looking intently at the wild tangle of plants and trees of the mangroves – the home of the Bengal tiger.

COURAGE does not always ROAR, sometimes it sounds like a gentle voice inside reminding you to face your fears.

Facts about Bengal tigers

- The Bengal tiger is the national animal of India and Bangladesh.
- Weighing up to 300 kilograms and measuring up to 3.3 metres in length, tigers are the largest wild cats in the world!
- Tigers like to hunt for food on their own at night.
- Unlike most cats, tigers like water and are very good swimmers.
- The roar of a tiger can be heard as far as 3 kilometres away.
- Each tiger has its own pattern of stripes. You will never find two tigers that look exactly the same.
- There are fewer than 2,500* Bengal tigers in the wild, making them an endangered species.
- A group of tigers is called a streak or an ambush of tigers.
- The Sundarbans – the mangrove forests where Bengal tigers are found – is increasingly threatened by rising sea levels caused by climate change.

*Numbers may vary.